To Your Good Health
A Russian Tale

retold by Jan M. Mike
illustrated by Deborah Healy

MODERN CURRICULUM PRESS
Pearson Learning Group

Long ago in old Russia, there lived a young man named Pavel. As a child, he had been a shoemaker's apprentice, and now he owned a little shop.

Now I must tell you that there was nothing at all out of the ordinary about Pavel. Oh, he was brave and strong, and clever and handsome. His eyes were bright blue and alive with curiosity. He could sing and play the flute like a master, and he crafted shoes and belts that made rich men and women weep with admiration. But Pavel was an ordinary man.

One day, as Pavel worked in his shop, the bell above the door rang. He looked up with a start. Standing before him was the czar's only daughter, Larissa. The czar was the king. Pavel knew enough to respect his superiors, so he jumped to his feet and bowed.

The czar's daughter smiled and turned to look over his wares. As Larissa examined purses, shoes, gloves, and belts, Pavel looked at her.

I must tell you that there was nothing out of the ordinary about Larissa either. Oh, her black eyes sparkled with intelligence and wit. She could ride the wildest horse and speak seven languages. She could play instruments and sing like a nightingale. But except for those things, Larissa was a very ordinary young woman.

Pavel showed Larissa a pair of fine dancing slippers, blue velvet crusted with tiny pearls. She looked up at him. Her eyes sparkled. They seemed to say, "I find you interesting. I would like to know you better."

Pavel smiled, and his eyes seemed to answer, "I find you beautiful and clever. I too would like to know you better."

Now, since their mouths said nothing beyond the ordinary, no one but they knew what their eyes had agreed to. Larissa took the dainty, delicate slippers and left the store. But she returned the next day, and the next.

A year passed. Larissa now owned 183 pairs of new shoes, sixty-seven new purses, forty-eight new belts, and sixty-two pairs of new gloves. When her father, the czar, received the shoemaker's bill, he decided that something had to be done.

Everyone agreed that the czar was an extraordinary man. As large and hairy as a wintering bear, he had the flaming temper of a wild boar, or pig. Every day he would issue new orders that no one dared disobey. He ruled the land with fear and fury.

The czar decreed it was time for Larissa to be married. Princes from around the world arrived at the palace. Some were fat, and others thin. Some were tall, and others short. Each begged permission to marry her, and each, in turn, she refused. Eventually the flood of princes slowed to a trickle. Then it stopped.

Pavel realized it was now his turn. Larissa had turned down all his superiors. That must mean that her eyes spoke the truth. But how could he, a mere shoemaker, gain permission to marry the only daughter of the czar?

The czar had ordered many laws passed, but the most foolish one was this: Each time the czar sneezed, bells rang across the land. People everywhere had to drop what they were doing and shout, "To your good health!" Shoemaker and shepherd, farmer and shopkeeper, all had to stop and shout, "To your good health!"

As Pavel tried to think of a way to bring himself to the czar's attention, the sneezing bells rang. Everyone stopped and shouted, "To your good health!"

Everyone, that is, but Pavel.

Immediately people noticed, and soon the royal guards were upon him. They dragged him to the royal palace and brought him to the throne room.

Pavel bowed. The czar bristled with anger, but Larissa, who was standing next to him, smiled. Most men would have been terrified, but not Pavel. He saw a chance to make the czar notice him.

"Did you not hear the royal sneezing bells?" the czar asked.

"Yes, I heard the bells, Your Royal Highness," Pavel answered.

"Do you know the law?" the czar demanded.

"Yes, I know the law, Your Extreme Mightiness," Pavel replied.

"Then say it," the czar shouted. "Say 'To your good health!' "

Pavel threw back his shoulders, standing tall. Here was his chance.

"Certainly, Your Very Great Greatness! To my good health!"

The czar turned red with rage.

"Are you a fool?" he demanded.

"No, I am not, Your Very Majestic Majesty," Pavel answered, bowing once more.

Larissa giggled behind her fan.

"How dare you disobey my law! It is not to *your* good health, it is to *my* good health! To my good health!" The czar pounded his chest.

"Very well, Your High and Mightiness, to my good health! Mine!" Pavel replied, pounding his own chest.

The czar's high minister tiptoed up to Pavel. In a very loud whisper he said, "If you do not say what the czar wishes to hear, he will order you killed."

"I will gladly say what the czar wishes to hear," Pavel answered. "I vow it. But first he must give me permission to marry Larissa."

Larissa laughed out loud.

"Oh, yes, Father. I will marry him," she cried out.

The czar turned purple with fury.

"No, you won't!" he shouted. "Throw this man into the bear cage!"

As the guards hauled him across the palace, it was clear to Pavel that he had made the czar notice him. So far, so good. Now if he could just survive the bear cage, perhaps he could make the czar like him.

The guards opened a large iron gate. They threw Pavel into a small room. The floor was covered with dirt, and the walls were cold and slimy.

A low growl rumbled through the little room. Pavel looked up as a very large bear rushed at him. Pavel's eyes opened wide and the bear stopped suddenly. Pavel closed his eyes and heard the bear growl again. Pavel's eyes flew open, and the bear took a step back.

For some reason the animal would not attack as long as Pavel stared at it. To survive, he would have to stare at the bear all night long.

As darkness fell, Pavel's eyelids grew heavy.
It had been an exciting day, and he was tired.
He slapped at his cheeks, then pinched his elbows.
He pulled his hair. He even bit his tongue. It was
going to be a very long night.

Then he heard a voice, a sweet and lovely voice
singing a loud, lively peasant tune. Larissa had
sneaked out of bed. She was sitting next to the bear
cage, singing.

"Do you often sing the bear to sleep?"
Pavel asked.

"All the time," Larissa answered. "Why don't you
sing with me?"

And so he did. All night long, Pavel and Larissa sang the loudest songs they knew. When dawn arrived, Larissa tiptoed away. Pavel stood and stretched, wide awake.

A few minutes later, the czar's high minister arrived. He looked quite surprised to see Pavel alive. Guards pulled the shoemaker from the bear cage. They gave him a crust of dry bread, a cup of warm water, and a rag to nap on. His liberty did not last, however. That evening they took him back to the czar.

The czar still looked angry as Pavel walked into the room. Larissa, sitting next to her father, winked at Pavel. He smiled at her.

"Well, young man," said the czar, "now you know how it feels to be close to death. Will you tell me what I wish to hear?"

"I'm not afraid of dying ten deaths, Your Most High and Mighty Excellence! I will say what you wish to hear only if you give me permission to marry Larissa."

"Oh, do give permission, Father," Larissa begged.

The czar ignored her. His cheeks were flaming with rage.

"How dare you disobey me when I issue an order? Ten deaths? I will show you ten deaths! Throw him into the boar pen."

The guards marched Pavel out of the room, down the hall, and past the bear cage. One guard opened a second iron gate and threw the shoemaker into the boar pen.

Ten wild boars crowded the little room, grunting and squealing. These were not sweet little pigs with pink skins and curly tails. They were huge, ferocious animals with sharp tusks and angry red eyes.

"Ten deaths," Pavel muttered. "Well, we'll see."

He grabbed his little silver flute out of his sleeve and began to play. Sweet music drifted upon the air.

The boars sniffed and snorted, squinting at the silver flute. Slowly, one boar stood on his hind legs and began to dance. Then another stood up, and another, until all the boars danced to the sound of the little silver flute.

Pavel wanted to laugh at the silly sight, but he knew if he took his mouth away from the flute, the boars would rush over to hurt him. An hour passed and his arms grew tired, but still he played.

"Well, this won't do at all."

Pavel looked up. Larissa stood outside the boar pen, holding her lute. He wanted to ask her what she meant, but he didn't dare stop playing.

"Here, let's try a faster tune," Larissa said, and she began to strum the lute's strings.

Pavel joined in, and as they played a lively tune, the boars began to dance even faster. Larissa and Pavel played for an hour or more, until all the boars collapsed in a snoring heap.

Larissa tiptoed off, carrying her lute. Pavel climbed to the top of the pile of snoring boars and fell fast asleep.

Early the next morning, the czar's high minister was quite surprised to find Pavel napping on a pile of exhausted boars. The guards woke him and dragged him from the cell, while the wild pigs continued to snore.

Once more Pavel was given bread and water. Since he wasn't tired this time, he spent the afternoon playing chess with the high minister. When evening came, the guards took him to the throne room.

The czar looked furious as Pavel walked into the room. Larissa, sitting next to her father, waved at Pavel. He grinned at her.

"Well," said the czar, "now you know how it feels to be close to ten deaths. Will you tell me what I wish to hear?"

"I'm not afraid of dying a hundred deaths, Your Extreme and Very Wise Excellence! I will say what you wish to hear only if you will give me permission to marry Larissa."

"Oh, please say yes this time, Father," Larissa begged.

The czar ignored her, his face red with fury.

"Once more you dare to disobey me when I issue an order. A hundred deaths? I will show you a hundred deaths! Throw him into the rat pit."

The guards marched Pavel out of the room, down the hall, past the bear cage and the boar pen. One guard opened a third iron gate and pushed the shoemaker into the rat pit.

Small furry rats nearly filled the little room. They climbed the walls and hung from the ceiling. The dim light reflected off their sharp teeth and claws.

"A hundred deaths!" Pavel muttered. "I have to learn to watch what I say."

He pulled out his flute, but the rats simply ignored him. As ten rats climbed up his left leg and twenty climbed up his right leg, Pavel kicked furiously. Two rats fell to his shoulders, clinging to his shirt. He tried to brush them away.

"Oh, the poor things look hungry."

Pavel looked over at the door, where Larissa stood holding a large picnic basket.

"I'm afraid that someone forgot to feed them," she continued, taking a large wheel of cheese out of the basket.

"I fear that you're right. May I help you?" Pavel asked.

She handed him two loaves of freshly baked bread, and they both set about feeding the rats.

An hour later, a hundred well-fed and happy rats dozed in a corner of the little room. Pavel and Larissa laughed as they ate cold chicken and the rest of the bread and cheese.

"Aha!"

Pavel looked up. There was the czar, standing over Larissa.

"I knew that someone was helping this disobedient young man! It was you, my daughter."

Pavel hastily stood and bowed. Larissa made a quick curtsey. "Father, don't be angry," she said. "I was simply feeding our guest."

For once the czar looked more thoughtful than angry. He pulled the key off the wall, and swung open the door.

"Come along, Pavel. You might as well come too, Larissa. I have thought of a way to get rid of this young man, once and for all."

Larissa followed the czar through empty halls lit by torches. Pavel trailed behind.

Finally they stopped in front of a golden door. The czar unlocked the door and opened it. Pavel and Larissa followed him inside.

The room was filled with treasure. Gold plates were stacked to the ceiling. Gold cups lined the walls. Diamond and ruby necklaces were piled in one corner, with sapphire and emerald bracelets in another. Huge teardrop-shaped pearls filled one chest and glittering rings were scattered on the floor.

"Here, young man. Take whatever you want, or take all of it. Simply tell me what I want to hear, and leave my daughter alone."

But Pavel shook his head. "I thank you for your kind offer, Your Most Generous Majesty. But all of the treasure in the world means less to me than a single hair on your daughter's head. You see, I love her."

"You love her! Well, why didn't you say that in the first place?"

The czar rubbed his eyes, then he pulled at his mustache. Finally he turned to his daughter.

"Well, my dear, do you love him? Is that why you keep helping him?"

"Yes, Father."

"And if I give you permission to get married," he looked up at Pavel, "will you promise to say what I want to hear?"

Pavel bowed, then he reached over and grabbed Larissa's hand. "Oh, yes. The very next time you sneeze, Your Majesty."

"Well, since you are willing to face a hundred deaths for her, and you won't give her up for all my treasure, and since you love her and she loves you, I suppose I must give you permission."

And so it came to be that Pavel and Larissa were married the very next day. The wedding was a small one, but the wedding feast was quite large.

Now I must tell you that the czar's cook was a very good cook except for one thing. She always used far too much pepper. So when she placed a large roast in front of the czar, and the czar took a long sniff, his nose began to twitch. Everyone sat quietly and watched as the czar's eyes watered and his whole face turned red. He sniffled. He snorted. Then he gave a huge, loud, royal sneeze.

Before the sneezing bells could ring, before anyone could say anything, Pavel leaped to his feet and shouted, "To your good health!"

And, I'm told, they all lived happily ever after.